THE MOSH PIT FROM HELL

STEFON MEARS

Also by Stefon Mears

The Rise of Magic Series
Magician's Choice
Sleight of Mind
Lunar Alchemy
Three Fae Monte
The Sphinx Principle
Double Backed Magic
Mercury Fold (forthcoming)

Cavan Oltblood Series
Half a Wizard
The Ice Dagger
Spells of Undeath

Power City Tales
Not Quite Bulletproof
No Money in Heroism

Standalones
The Mosh Pit from Hell
The Hireling
The Captain's Cat
Save Whiskers!
The Ogre of Threepeaks
Between the Cracks
Sects and the City
Prince of a Thousand Worlds
Devil's Night
Portal-Land, Oregon
Stealing from Pirates
Fade to Gold
With a Broken Sword
Twice Against the Dragon
The House on Cedar Street
Sudden Death
On the Edge of Faerie

Short Story Collections
Spell Slingers
Twisted Timelines
Longhairs and Short Tales: A Collection of Cat Stories
Dangerous Space
Confronting Legends (Spells & Swords Vol. 1)
The Patreon Collection, Vol. 1-8 (Vol. 9, coming soon)

Nonfiction
The 30-Day Novel and Beyond!

Spells for Hire Series
Devil's Shoestring
Zombie Powder
Spirit Trap
Dragon's Blood

The Telepath Trilogy
Surviving Telepathy
Immoral Telepathy
Targeting Telepathy

Edge of Humanity Series
Caught Between Monsters
Hunting Monsters

Jumpstart Duchy Series
Into the Torn Kingdoms
The Dragon's Gold
The Gift Castle
The Deadly Feast
The King's Test
Triumph in the Torn Kingdoms

Published by Thousand Faces Publishing, Portland, Oregon

http://1kfaces.com

ISBN: 978-1-948490-53-5

1

I woke up backstage, but that didn't tell me what world I was in.

Lots of bands. Lots of worlds. Lots of … mes.

The area around me was pretty dark, and while my eyes adjusted, I could hear the sounds of stage prep underway. Roadies have a language all their own. It's half-grunts, half-monosyllables, with complexity strewn in through head bobs, pointing with shoulders and elbows, and gestures that could be useful, or obscene, or somehow both.

Don't get me wrong. I'm not dissing them. Roadies aren't some kind of troglodyte creatures — which are always heavy into drums, if you ever have to play for them. No. It's just that roadies are always doing about a dozen things at once. Those who can't handle it burn out while they're still speaking full sentences on the job.

The ones who stick with it, they don't have time for elucidation. So they communicate with swift efficiency, using their whole bodies and only as much verbalization as is entirely necessary to do the job.

God love the roadies. They keep the music flowing.

These roadies were bringing in gear and setting up a drum kit.

With attendant swearing and accidental splash cymbals. Which told me two things.

First, I had a gig coming soon. Which meant I needed to figure out where I was and what I was playing. Prestissimo.

Second, I'd be playing with one of my bands. Currently — assuming reasonably similar timestreams, which was a big assumption, I know — I had about sixteen different bands I performed with across various worlds.

What those bands were doing — what those *worlds* were doing — while I was elsewhere was one of those questions I'd long ago learned not to ask.

Oh, I could get an answer. If I managed to ask the right venue manager. Some of them were on the inside, and knew all the ins and outs. But the ones that didn't know would invariably think me an idiot and try to shaft the band on our fee. Which I *would not* tolerate.

And the ones who *did* know what was going on weren't much better. They'd tend to smile and nod, and say something annoying like, "Oh, I could tell you. But then you'd have to think about it when you're someplace else, wouldn't you?" Or "If you were ready to understand that, you'd be in management." Or "You just keep your focus on the music. Leave the petty details to us paper pushers."

Venue managers. If I have a curse, they're it.

My eyes had adjusted enough to make out my surroundings now, mostly in shades of gray.

Rafters up above me. Steel girders that looked a few decades old. Fluorescent bulb lights — off at the moment — dangling from cheap chain links. HVAC duct tubes and way too many extension cords to be safe, if any decent fire department ran a spot check.

Some version of the ... 1970s or later, but that was about all I could tell. Not yet that point in the ... 2030s or so when even venues like this one switched from fluorescents to LEDs, or something similar.

I was lying down on a stack of equipment crates. Hardcases. Gray with steel trim. The kind that would have what they held and who they belonged to stenciled on the side in white.

These were empty. I could tell by how easily they shifted underneath me, if I moved my hips a little.

Made my position a little precarious, but I wasn't ready to get down yet. I needed more information.

Unfortunately, that also meant I couldn't risk *looking* down.

See, roadies at work don't stop moving. Which meant they'd come and go from this area on a steady basis, whether it was lit up or not. Might come in any moment.

Right now, they'd be ignoring me. Assuming I'm just another singer who partied too hard before a gig — which I would *never* do, by the way. I respect the music and the audience too much for that, to say nothing of my bandmates — and not someone worth waking up until closer to showtime.

But if I look down, they might realize I'm awake. Then they'd tell someone, and things I wasn't ready for would start happening.

So I lay there, and tried to figure out more of what I could get from where I was.

The air smells took me a moment to parse. Someone had been spot-welding recently, and some of the dust in the air back here still had that gas-cooked smell. That wasn't all, though. Oil and gas odors, which suggested I was in the loading area, but not strong, which meant that the dock bay door was closed.

Explained the lack of fresher air, too.

Under that, though, duct tape. Lots of it.

Duct tape's smell is distinctive, once you know it. And I'd been around a *lot* of duct tape, through the years.

The odor is ... kind of gummy. And if you spend enough time around it, when you smell it, the scent just kind of gloms onto the top of your mouth, and spreads around. Which is just *so* much worse when your mouth is already dry from an unexpected world jump.

Which my mouth was just then.

This was old duct tape, though. Not the fresh stuff that the roadies would be breaking out soon to keep all of tonight's cables under control. Soon as I could get any other taste in my mouth — even water'd be good — the duct tape taste would pass.

Time to get down.

I made a show of yawning and moaning a little, as though I had a splitting headache. The hardcases trembled when I did, but long as I moved slow enough, I'd be fine.

A roadie hustled through on a mission. Male. Beefy. Bushy blonde hair. Like maybe he'd been a Viking in another life. In this one, he was wearing a black tee shirt that read Parkway Theater on the back. His jeans were ... was that acid wash?

So, late '80s or early '90s then.

He noticed me, but only to say, "Band soundcheck's in twenty, dickhead."

Then he was ripping open some cabinet and digging out about two miles of mic cord. Thus burdened, he hustled out of the room again.

Wasn't personal, by the way. The "dickhead" bit. Probably his name for any performer he didn't know until he had a reason to be nice to them. I'd give him one later.

Always be good to the roadies. Always. Not just nice. It's not about just being polite. You don't just *say* "thank you." You *mean* it. And it helps if you give them a case of beer, for after.

This particular roadie had given me an important point of information, though. First, because he spoke English. Second, because "dickhead" was a very American insult. Third, because his accent was pure West Coast. Which narrowed things down to ... most likely, California, Oregon or Washington.

Yes, Alaska was possible, but unless it was high summer, I'd probably need more clothing...

Right. Time to finally look down and see what I was wearing. Whatever it was didn't feel like much.

Sounds odd, right? Waiting that long to check out my own clothes?

Here's the thing, though. Whenever I got to a new world, first thing I had to do — always — was figure out *something* about where and when I was. And most times, my clothes were just show costumes that wouldn't tell me within *forty years* of when I was, let alone where.

So I usually waited.

Plus, less chance of shock, if it was something outrageous.

Pretty sedate this time. What there was of it. Pretty sure the t-shirt had once been an Aerosmith concert shirt, and the pants had started life as pale blue acid wash jeans.

Both were now so torn up that I had at least as much skin showing as cloth. Probably more.

Good thing I kept my body trim. Never yet shown up anyplace where the body was a surprise. Though that just made things awkward, those times when I was performing for people who weren't human.

Like those troglodytes. That was less a case of "play for your supper" than "play or *be* supper."

I had some "jewelry" this time, though. Leather wristbands, studded with pointy chrome. Kind of went with the motorcycle boots, also studded with pointy chrome. And I was pretty sure the boots had steel toes.

Well, at least if I got into a fight, I'd be armed.

Now, though, it was time for me to find out more about where I was and who I was playing with.

With any luck, maybe I'd even find out why I was here.

2

———————

THERE'S A TRICK TO CLIMBING DOWN A STACK OF EMPTY MUSICAL equipment hardcases.

See, the bottom level is always on wheels. They're the bigger, wider cases that held parts of the drum kit, or effects units and the like. And those things would be more than happy to roll different directions and spill my silly ass all over the concrete. Which I could not afford.

I don't mean in terms of healthcare, either. Though that might be a bitch of its own, depending on a few factors. No, I mean that I had the band's soundcheck in a little under twenty minutes, and whatever need had brought me to this time and place, it wasn't to crack my skull open in the loading bay.

Then again, maybe it was. Maybe I was here to die and get off this particular merry-go-round.

Well, if so, at least I'd get this gummy, dusty duct tape taste out of my mouth. Blessing and the curse of that wonderful stuff. Thousands of uses, but once you really know the smell...

Anyway, the trick to getting down safely is to not let your weight swing side to side. Not hard, but it does take a little practice.

See, the way most people go about something like this, they bring one foot down onto a latch or handle, and let their weight come down with it. And that's how ribs and hips get bruised by unforgiving concrete.

Now, one way to avoid this is to go down by the end of stack, instead of in the middle. But this particular stack was against the wall, and off each end was another stack of hardcases, not quite my body width away.

No route down there. But I could use that wall to my advantage.

So instead I knelt on the top with my boots hanging off the edge, facing the nasty old hardwood of a wall that had seen more scuffs and wounds than a battlefield.

Crouching down, I reached both hands down my sides, for the first handles I could come to.

Once I had a decent grip, I kicked out backwards.

Tricky part here? Holding my head back so my face didn't kiss the steel of the edge before my feet swung down into the sides of lower cases. Driving them back into the wall.

Short drop down to the concrete and I was good.

Good enough to get a slow clap from someone behind me.

"Not bad. Can't give you more than a seven-point-five, though. Didn't stick the landing."

A woman's voice, dripping with sarcasm.

"Come on," I said, turning around. "Don't I get anything extra for the kick-out? I mean, that was going above and beyond. I could've just let my feet slide down."

The woman was a bartender. A pro. I knew it at once. Pro bartenders, they all have this *look*. Or maybe it's something in their aspect. When they're on-site, it's like every time they look at you, they can tell exactly how much you've had to drink.

Oh, maybe not in an absolute sense, but in terms of your body-weight and tolerance, they can peg you to the ounce.

They can also tell how much trouble they think you'll be.

This particular bartender was a bottle blonde, in *maybe* her early thirties. Hair teased out high enough to require half a can of Aquanet. Her jeans were more slashed than torn, and her Parkway Theater black tee had been chopped in half to show off her toned and tanned midriff.

She had the kind of looks that said she got great tips, at the price of getting hit-on nonstop from opening to closing. But something about her posture said she wouldn't hesitate to eighty-six anyone who crossed a line with her.

Including some singer pulling jackass stunts in the loading bay.

She gave a good kind of considering frown while she contemplated the extra effort in my descent, then gave me an evil smile and shook her head.

"Without that kick-out, you'd be lucky to rate a five."

"Sure you're not the Russian judge?"

She scoffed. "Russian judge wouldn't give you more than a three, *with* the kick-out."

I definitely had the place and timeline about right then. Russian judge jokes related to that kind of scoring were big along the West Coast of the United States around then.

To say nothing of the clothes.

"You must be Leon, right?" she said. "The singer?"

"That's me," I said. Name didn't tell me anything, by the way. My name is always a version of Leon, or something close to it along the "lion" theme.

"All right," she said. "I'll tell *you* and you tell your band. I hear you sold all your tickets. Good job. Pay to play sucks, but it's what we're all stuck with." She raised a halting hand. "Doesn't mean you guys drink free. You each get one," — she held up one long index finger — "*one* beer of your choice on the house. Anything else, gotta pay cash for. Got me?"

"Got you," I said, with a nod for emphasis. "I'll make sure they know."

"Good," she said, turning away.

"What's your name?"

She turned back, giving me a look that said she had a lecture on deck about how she doesn't date musicians.

I showed her the no-threat empty hands.

"I just think it'd be rude to call you 'bartender' all night."

She narrowed her eyes like this was a trick. And honestly, she probably had reason to be suspicious. Bands around then — especially lead singers — all had the rep of being serious alley cat sluts.

Not judging, you understand. People who love sex should be free to enjoy it all they want, and gods know I've enjoyed my share.

But I could completely understand how the reputation could leave a hot — or rather *fine*, to use a colloquialism from the right timeline — bartender suspicious.

Finally, she gave me a tentative nod.

"You can call me Trish," she said.

"Thank you, Trish. I'll make sure my boys behave themselves."

She didn't say anything to that. Just gave me a disbelieving look as she turned away.

To emphasize my point, I did *not* watch her walk away. In case she checked.

Just goes to show the sacrifices I am willing to make in the name of music.

Speaking of my bandmates, though, they had to be around here somewhere. And I still needed something to get that gummy-dusty taste out of my mouth. But before I went looking, I needed to know...

Ah. There it was, stenciled on the side of a hardcase: TPA.

That was us. The Trash Pandas of the Apocalypse.

3

——————

Ah, pay-to-play.

Remember how I said that if I have a curse, it's venue managers? Yeah. Pay-to-play is just one of the many forms of evil they have wrought through the years.

The whole concept just...

Give me a second.

All right.

Now.

The idea goes like this.

Band: "Hi! We're a new group of awesome musicians who can blow the roof off your establishment. We'd love to audition for you, and maybe line up a few gigs."

Evil Venue Manager: "That's all right, Band. Your demo sounds good enough. No audition necessary."

B: "Whoohoo! Yes! When can we play?"

EVM: "I've got an open slot for you to be the first act of three, next Tuesday. You'd go on at eight, and play a twenty-minute set."

B: "Well, a Tuesday's not ideal, but we know we've gotta pay our dues. We'll take it."

EVM: "Excellent! I'll put you down. If that show works out, we'll get you into our regular rotation. Oh, and it'll be two hundred dollars."

B: "All right! Our first paid gig! We're on our way!"

EVM: "You misunderstand me. I'm not paying *you* two hundred dollars. You're paying *me* two hundred dollars."

B: "Excuse me?"

EVM: "Oh, this is great for you though!"

B: "How is paying you two hundred dollars great for us?"

EVM: "For that two hundred dollars, you get *four hundred dollars* worth of our ten dollar admission tickets. All you have to do is sell them to forty of your fans, and we *each* make *two hundred dollars!*"

B: "We don't have fans yet. We haven't played any gigs."

EVM: "So you discount the tickets and offer people a deal. Lots of bands do that."

B: "Offer discounts? So, cut our pay, while you make the same money? And if we can't sell enough, we pay the difference?"

EVM: "Gotta hustle to eat in this world, Band."

B: "But ... you have an established customer base. And you make most of your money selling drinks. While *we* provide the entertainment..."

EVM: "Lots of bands want to play here. Take it or leave it."

I'd like to think that whoever came up with the pay-to-play scheme is burning in some kind of hell. Alongside all the venue managers who happily instituted it, and people who block doorways and grocery store aisles to hold extended conversations.

Now, Trish had mentioned pay-to-play, and that we'd sold all our tickets. So we had a pretty good fan base going.

That told me one thing, and gave me two questions.

It told me where I'd landed in TPA's cycle. Right now, we're one of the headlining acts on the club scene, which meant I was in the San Francisco Bay Area, sometime during ... 1990, I think. Summer, if I had to guess.

First question — what the hell venue was this?

If you hadn't guessed by the way I was dressed, TPA was a hard rock / heavy metal outfit, falling somewhere on the rock spectrum between Guns 'N Roses and Iron Maiden.

I remember all the main hard rock and metal clubs around the Bay Area at that time. The Stone. The Omni. Cactus Club. Niles Station. Maybe three or four others.

None of them, however, were called the Parkway Theater. So that was weird.

Second question — where were the other bands?

The pay-to-play clubs never had only one band in their shows. Even when a big name band came through — or a band big enough to headline, but too small for amphitheaters and major event centers — the ticket had at *least* one local opening act. Usually two or three. The big name band would make its guarantee, which might include a cut of the door — plus merch sales — and the others would all be pay-to-play.

There wasn't enough gear back here in the loading bay for multiple bands. But my band's soundcheck was in less than twenty minutes. Which meant either that there was a big headliner and we were the only opening act — a possibility, if the headliner was someone big enough — or something screwy was going on.

And if there was a headliner that wasn't us, where were they? A touring band should have been here a couple of hours before any real soundchecks were done. Or at least their *gear* should've been. And I should've seen the headliner's roadies running around in tour shirts, not the venue's.

And if *we* were the headliners, where were the opening acts?

This was not adding up.

I spared a glance for the stage, where roadies were mucking about with the monitors and stacks and even more miles of cable than I could see among the extension cords in the rafters.

Couldn't go out onto the stage while they were that busy. I'd get in somebody's way.

Houselights were up, though, so I could see a couple of details that might become important.

The main floor didn't have any tables. All open SRO. But there was a balcony tracing three — no *four* walls. This place was pentagonal, which was weird, but not equilateral at least, which would be *too* weird.

This design was more like the way a kid draws houses. Three sides like it's going to be a square, but instead of the square's fourth side, it got an angle for a roof.

Past the buzzing cloud of roadies, I could see the drum kit well enough to know it was Danny's. Danny was TPA's drummer and a founding member, and I'd've known his kit even without the stylized TPA on the kick.

Danny used five toms. More than most drummers. Three big, two small. Practically his signature.

Unfortunately, even standing *near* the stage entrance was starting to get me glares from the busy roadies, though, so I backed off and went looking for the green room. Or whatever they'd call it in this place. The room where the band would be waiting.

4

I DIDN'T MEET ANYONE WHILE LOOKING FOR THE BAND, WHICH MIGHT'VE been the weirdest thing yet. I mean, yeah, the roadies were busy on stage, but there was *nobody* else back here?

Clubs always seemed to have *someone* around. Waitstaff coming on or going off shift or on break would be the most common. Most clubs put the "employee breakroom" — read, the dirty room with the cheap table, chairs, microwave and, if you're very lucky, a fridge — close-ish to the band's green room.

Often they regretted that choice, those times when their waitstaff proved excessively interested in one of the bands. Or at least in one of the people *in* one of the bands.

But in general, design efficiency was king. So the employee restrooms, green room, and breakroom would all be close together.

And yet, I didn't see or hear *any*one as I descended the concrete stairs that would lead me to the green room. Just those roadies working up on the stage.

At least I smelled old beer, stale smoke and a hint of urine. Otherwise I would've started thinking this wasn't a club at all. That maybe I'd entered some kind of *Spinal Tap* hell and I'd spend eternity wandering through the backstage area, looking for a stage I'd never find.

The green room, when I found it, was actually pretty good.

Not just one thrift-store-special couch, but two! By the way, you don't ever want to see those things under a black light. There's not enough bleach in the world.

Fortunately, the lights in here weren't black, but incandescent. Four bare bulbs behind a wire grate in the center of the ceiling.

Walls were covered in fliers and posters from past gigs, but instead of the usual torn or scrawled-on paper, these were all behind plastic.

Not formal frames, you understand. That would cost *money*. No, someone had put up a bunch of old fliers and posters and then slapped up sheet plastic over them, screwing the plastic directly into the lime green concrete.

Yes. This was a literal green room. So someone must've had aspirations toward comedy.

But the *pièce de résistance* was the spread. Two whole tables of it. Four boxes of delivery pizza still warm enough that I could smell them. Bottles of water and cans of soda sitting in plastic tubs of ice.

True, for a big-name, touring band, this spread would be a joke. But bands like us didn't get detailed contracts that let us specify the color of our M&Ms. Trust me. For a club band of that era, what I saw there was strictly top-of-the-line.

I grabbed a water and a slice of pepperoni. Wasn't even bottom-of-the-barrel pizza. It had *taste*. I mean, good cheese *and* good pepperoni. Well worth the grease, especially to chase away that lingering dust and duct-tape nonsense.

I'd downed half my slice before turning to check on my bandmates.

One of the nice things about playing with a band. I wouldn't be surrounded by strangers all night. I knew everyone in sixteen-odd of my bands.

Danny was sprawled across one of the couches, air drumming what looked like "Four Sticks" by Led Zeppelin. Which meant he was most of the way through his personal pre-concert routine. He'd finish with "YYZ" by Rush.

I never knew exactly how much Danny ate, but it had to have been a lot. Drummers burn more calories per practice, rehearsal and gig than anyone else. But Danny was still a heavy dude. And with his bushy brown hair and beard — not to mention all the hair on those muscled arms — he could pass for a Bigfoot in the right lighting.

Stevie was practically Danny's opposite. Take a proportionally normal — if pale — dude about five feet tall and stretch him until he's six-four, give him pale blond hair that falls to the bottom of his ribcage and you've got Stevie. Skinny enough to hide behind a mic stand, but scary good on lead guitar. And I don't just mean he played ultra fast. He didn't. But Stevie, his sense of timing, intonation and musicality was so good I could only compare him to the likes of Mozart.

Sometimes, live, I'd throw Stevie a solo out of the blue. He never failed to improvise something so incredible the crowd would lose its mind.

Stevie was in the middle of his own pre-show routine. Facing the corner. His Gibson Les Paul Starburst plugged into his big head-phones while he had his eyes closed and both hands on his fretboard, harmonizing two different sets of scales at the same time in what looked like waltz time.

Greg had to be around here somewhere, though. I could hear the ticking of his unamplified bass.

Hard to miss Greg. Dark skin with lots of tattoos and a jolt of short dreads surrounding a face that was usually smiling wide.

Oh. Of course. Soon as I thought of it, I knew where he'd be, and a quick check told me I was right.

He was lying on his back *under* the spread tables, as close to in his own world as he could get. Bass in hand. Not even plugged into head-phones while he alternated bars from Rush, Primus, Police, Bob Marley and Metallica.

Greg was a madman, but he played a hell of a bass.

No Ian, though, which resolved my final timeline question.

Ian joined us in September of 1990, and proved to be the final puzzle piece that got TPA signed to a major label and opening for serious big-name acts.

See, Stevie and Greg were both terrific players, but to tie them together they really needed a strong rhythm player. I could handle it — and then some — but doing so limited my options as a singer.

Ian made the difference there. As a rhythm player, Ian was an irresistible force. Kept Stevie and Greg anchored, in those moments when the call of the muse might otherwise overwhelm them.

Plus, he let me put the guitar down — live, at least — and focus on frontman stuff. Moving around more. Interacting with the audience. That kind of thing.

The addition of Ian elevated us to the next level.

So if Ian wasn't with us yet, this was most likely late spring or summer 1990. I'd need to remember that, if it became important.

Strange, the little details that mattered, whenever I showed up someplace like this.

I didn't just hop worlds every day, you see. I'd often get to settle in someplace for a week, a month, a year or two even, before it happened again.

But wherever I went, there was a reason for it. Something I needed to do. And when I did, sometimes I got to go back where I'd been. Other times, I just had to settle in and wait for the next jump.

But talking to my bandmates during their pre-show routines was a no-no. So I settled in and started my own vocal exercises while I looked for my cherry red Gibson Flying V.

Found it on a stand behind the couches and out of the way.

I strapped it on and added my fingering warmups to my vocal exercises.

It was time to get ready for my gig. Whatever it was.

5

———————

I DON'T MIND ADMITTING I GOT LOST IN MY WARMUP EXERCISES. I MEAN, part of being who I am meant I was always gig-ready when I showed up someplace. If I'd had to walk out of that loading bay straight onto stage and start singing, I'd've nailed my performance and left them wanting more.

It's what I do.

But give me a chance to go through warmups, and it's like I'm fourteen again, figuring all these things out for the first time. Reveling in the sound of my voice as I move through scales, runs and jumps. I'm a natural baritone, but trained enough to sing any tenor or bass part I need to. Which makes just playing with my voice a lot of fun.

And on the guitar side, I never quite got over the thrill of watching my own fingers produce the sounds I knew so well from records.

That's right. When I was a kid and first developing all this, we listened to records. As in LPs. As in wax. As in the things that held off the assaults of eight-tracks and cassettes, but finally lost out to compact discs, only to stage a comeback few saw coming around the time that most listeners were settling for electronic files.

Audiophiles. Very grass-is-always-greener, you know?

So I was deep in my own world of fun with notes and sounds when someone yelled out, *"HEY, DICKHEADS!"*

Now, it's one thing to get called "dickhead" by a roadie in a hurry. It's something else entirely to have it yelled at you while you're warming up for a gig.

I turned an album-cover worthy don't-fuck-with-me look on the speaker, and so did my bandmates.

The guy who'd yelled it at us was no roadie. Oh, he had the jeans and tee-shirt, but he didn't have the *look*. He was a decade too old, and the extra time had stolen half his hair, and what was left was stringy. Though he'd gamely put what brown locks he had in a pony-tail that was just sad.

Plus, he had a clipboard in his hand. And rare was the roadie who picked one of those up, much less carried it around like it was both weapon and shield.

He was holding it up like a shield right now, as he saw our expressions.

He didn't apologize though. Which just proved that either a) he wasn't very smart, b) he was part of venue management — stage manager maybe — or c) all of the above.

He did start talking though. So maybe he had *some* smarts to him.

"You guys are due onstage for your sound check. Miss it and I don't want to hear about anyone bitching to our engineer about your sound tonight."

We didn't say anything. Didn't need to. Plus, we'd been a unit long enough to have established procedures for when someone pissed us off, collectively.

We strutted past him.

Stevie first. Too skinny to be properly threatening, but tall enough to loom anyway. And he wiped his strings while he walked as though polishing a literal axe, rather than a figurative one.

Greg went next, as big a contrast to Stevie's pale ass as we had. Which meant that if Mr. Hey Dickheads was racist, Danny and I would see some tell. Which would make things worse for him.

He gave Greg more room, but that was it. And Greg needed more room. Like me, he stays toned and trim, but he's got bigger arms and shoulders.

So at least Mr. Hey Dickheads wasn't racist. Which meant I didn't crank my dark look up a few notches as I moved past him. Though I did notice his skin had a dark, yellowish cast to it. Liver problems, maybe. Not a good sign at his age.

Didn't look back to see what Danny did, but I smiled a little when I heard Mr. Hey Dickheads' breath catch.

"Remind me," I said to Greg. "Just where the fuck *are* we, anyway?"

"Park—"

"You know what I mean."

Greg gave me an even wider smile than normal, and clapped his hand on my shoulder. "My friend, you have the extraordinary pleasure of joining us as we open a brand new club. First band, first headliner, first everything."

He jerked his head back toward Mr. Hey Dickheads.

"Must be why jerkface is a *wee* bit stressed."

"In his defense," Stevie said, "he'd probably tried getting our attention three or four times before yelling."

"And his luck would've been better," Danny piped in, "if he'd toggled the light switch instead."

"New club, eh?" I said with a smile. Sure, that sounded like the kind of thing that might be enough to pop me in from another world. I mean, I didn't remember any Parkway Theater, but this might be a splinter point.

See, lots of the worlds out there are just like ... well ... *your* world, I guess. I mean, I'm not sure *I* really have a world I can think of as mine anymore.

Point is, a lot of them come across as so similar because, once upon a time, they were only one world.

But then something happened. Something big enough to split one world into two.

There are lots of big examples. Worlds where the U.S. stayed neutral during WWII, and worlds where they annexed Japan and made it a state.

Those are the big forks.

But the little forks, they happened too, once worlds started splitting off a base. And some worlds could split over small things.

In one world, a minor league baseball player gets hot when he gets his chance during a September call-up and becomes a Major League regular for a decade. In another, he's hit by a pitch, fractures part of his hand, and gets forgotten.

In one world, a small-town girl becomes a Hollywood mainstay as a character actor. In another, she never leaves the farm.

Little things, that have ramifications of some sort. Though I admit, I've never been able to tell what the threshold is for splitting worlds. What size or type of event is needed to make it happen.

But a new club opening up could do it. Especially if that club went on to shift the Bay Area music scene at a time when it was really jumping. Like it was that year.

"But where *is* this club exactly? I got distracted on the drive in."

"Yeah," Danny said with a smile. "I saw her too. Like an ad for bicycle fitness. Or maybe for tights. Or—"

"Down, boy," Greg said, laughing. "She's gone now, and we, we are *here*."

"And where is here?" I asked.

"Why your favorite place in the world. The DMZ!"

6

———

I DON'T HAVE ANYTHING *AGAINST* MILPITAS, PER SE. I MEAN, AS FAR AS Bay Area suburbs go, it's definitely one of them. It just always seemed ... I don't know ... nondescript to me. Just another collection of tract houses and strip malls, with nothing that leapt out at me as a defining or interesting feature.

I mean, Foster City had those waterways. Fremont had a bridge. And Milpitas had...

Yeah.

So ... well ... somewhere along the lines, I began to joke that it didn't really exist.

I mean, *obviously* there were freeway exits and apartment complexes and Burger Kings and all that jazz. But my joke was that Milpitas wasn't actually a *town* or *city*.

The way I figured it, San Jose and Fremont had fought one long, knock-down drag-out war. The kind that lasted for years, until one day they decided that their people needed a break. But they weren't ready for full, formal peace talks to settle the great dispute between them.

(No, I never formally decided what that dispute was. But most of the time, when I told it, the dispute had to do with BART trains and whether or not San Jose would accept a station.)

So they'd settled for an armistice. And declared a demilitarized zone between them A DMZ that the rest of the world called...

Milpitas.

Because when they first established it, it was said to be a thousand paces across.

I don't know. It amused me. And it amused some girlfriends. And my bandmates got a kick out of it.

But a rock and metal club opening up there? Could draw a lot of south bay traffic. Could become a very big deal.

Maybe that was why I was here? Because this club would either stand or fall based on tonight's show?

Oh, that was rough.

I mean, on the one hand, if it failed, that meant *I* failed, and more importantly, my *band* failed.

But if it succeeded, that meant I'd have to keep coming to Milpitas...

No. No. I'd have to give it my all anyway. The band deserved it. The concertgoers deserved it. And if this meant I'd have to go to Milpitas more often, well, that would just be my cross to bear. I'd survive.

Now, a band's soundcheck varies, depending on the stage that band is at.

If you're still first act on a Tuesday night bill, you get a few minutes to make sure there are no dead mics or cables and your effects units are working. That's about it.

If you're one of the big headliners, your band soundcheck might require a full run-through. Because you're not *just* checking levels, you're checking levels all over the stage. And you're double-checking any fancy light gimmicks, the timing of any pyrotechnics and so forth. Almost like a mellow version of the concert itself.

The Trash Pandas of the Apocalypse, that night, were somewhere in the nebulous middle ground.

We got to go through a few songs, checking out both out sound levels and tuning while three of us moved around the stage and Danny checked varying amounts of pressure on his drumheads for both tuning and sound quality through the mixer.

Once that was done, we verbally ran through the set list while the lights person — a heavyset woman named Bella — double-checked timing of the few special lighting effects we got to use.

We were still at the stage where our shows were *about* our performance, not how we could *enhance* our performance, if that makes sense.

As we went through it all, I started to see a comforting sign.

Actual people.

Well, not that roadies weren't *actual people*. I just mean I was seeing people whose jobs weren't about setting up our gear or getting our asses on the stage.

You know. These were the *other* people who worked here.

Yes, I'd met Trish the Bartender. But the lack of other staff had been bugging me more than a little.

During our band soundcheck...

Oh. In case you don't know, I say it that way to differentiate it from the *final* soundcheck, which will be done by roadies, making sure nothing has gone wrong and that all the levels are coming across as the sound engineer expects them to.

Anyway, during our band soundcheck I started seeing the people in dark yellow shirts that read SECURITY in big black letters. Mostly guys, but a few women. About eight, all told. Most of them new enough at the gig that they watched us on the stage.

Not a good sign, that. That suggested that some of them had never worked security before. Which meant that this show was probably their first. Which made me wonder what kind of training, if any, they'd gotten before being handed their yellow shirts.

Had to hope it was more than just, "Look tough and toss the troublemakers."

Good security people knew how to deescalate problems and how to handle drunks — both the ones that just needed to sit for a second and the ones that needed to get bounced out hard before they did something violent or ugly.

Good security people could make or break a venue. If they were power-tripping, word would get around and the crowd would thin within a few shows until the place was just this side of a ghost town. At least, unless the club had something seriously good going for it.

And in the case of the Parkway Theater, *location* sure wouldn't be the draw.

If the security people were good, though, they could make the crowd feel safe while handling any problems quickly and quietly enough that most people wouldn't know there'd been a problem in the first place.

I'd have to keep an eye on them. If I was here to make sure this place hit, I couldn't let a few undertrained security types ruin it.

7

———————

Have to admit. Whoever ran the Parkway Theater might have skimped on hiring experienced security, but they hired a first-rate engineer. Most band soundchecks I've done in clubs like that one left me gritting my teeth over some technical point that either the engineer wasn't good enough to understand, or was too arrogant to listen to any opinion but his or her own.

This guy, though, he had his shit together. Had a rough level established before we even hit the stage. And though we'd had to change out one mic and three mic cords during the check, he kept things moving along the whole time.

Oh, that mic cord's bad? Well, let's just check on the bass while they fix it.

Very professional. By the end, I'd only raised five things that could have been considered questions or points for consideration. And he'd addressed all five without issue, adjusting three to suit our needs as a band, and explaining why the other two would be better the way they were, in this venue.

And he never raised his voice. Not once. Had to be the most Zen sound guy I'd ever met. Especially for an engineer about to open a new club with live music.

(Well, technically speaking I hadn't actually *met* him yet. But you know what I mean. Heck, the only reason I knew it was a "he" was the timbre of his voice. Because if a woman got stuck with a voice that deep, well, I could only hope for her sake that she'd be able to steer into it.)

As much as the security team worried me, the engineer relaxed me. If the sound and show were good enough, even a few bad security apples wouldn't give the club a black mark on its opening night.

And I was betting that Trish the Bartender noticed the security guys watching the stage when they should've been prepping for the doors to open. So maybe she'd be able to help management cull the herd a bit.

Assuming this wasn't just management cutting costs. Vis-à-vis, my point about evil venue managers.

Still, as we came off stage, the four of us were feeling good about that night's show. Positive enough, in fact, that even the sight of Mr. Hey Dickheads waiting for us in the green room didn't diminish our smiles.

"All right," he said, giving us what he probably thought was a winning smile, but really, just looked like indigestion. "It's just after six o'clock now. Doors open at seven. There'll be a couple of little preshow things you can come up for or not as you choose. But be ready to hit the stage at eight. And I mean eight *sharp*. None of that rockstar make-them-wait-for-us crap here. Got me?"

"Gotcha," Danny said with a grin. "We go on at eight-fifteen. Eight-thirty at the *latest*."

Mr. Hey Dickheads' narrow nostrils flared in what must've passed for a deep breath. For him.

"No," he started carefully, but Greg waved him off with a much more persuasive winning smile.

"Don't worry, Mr. Man," Greg said. "When the clock strikes eight, we'll already be in the wings and ready to blow the roof off this place."

Mr. Hey Dickheads' eyes narrowed suspiciously.

"I'm just fucking with you, man," Danny said, still grinning. "That's what *dickheads* do, right?"

Huh. Who'd've thought this guy's eyes could narrow further. Hard to believe he could see us just then. But he gave a sharp nod all the same. Then one more just like it, before he turned and strode quickly out of the room.

To his credit, he was walking away and not talking all that loud when he said, "You fucking well better be."

That set off a round of the kind of laughter that probably didn't help the guy's stress levels. But hey, he started it.

Then it was a waiting game. Eating was a bad idea at that point. I didn't need to be onstage with a belly full of pepperoni. Danny took a different view — and three slices — but that was Danny.

Greg and Stevie both retreated to their own worlds, doing more warm-ups, but I had a wander itch. I wanted to know more about this place. Why this theater might be important enough to get me to pop in.

If, in fact, it was the theater I was here for. Which I still didn't know.

So I checked the still too-empty hallway. No sign of anyone yet, which was just weird. But then, maybe whatever waitstaff they had was all helping set up the bar and such. I could hear the echoes of activity up above, but distant. No details.

The light down here in the concrete hallway...

That was another weird thing, now that I thought about it. I was in a basement. In the Bay Area.

The San Francisco Bay Area did not build basements. Oh, you could find a few here and there, I suppose, but they were always the exception. And strange.

This was earthquake country. And if the year was 1990, which I thought it was, then the whole area had just been through the Loma Prieta quake maybe nine months ago.

Which meant either this was a new building entirely — and some fool hadn't learned their lesson when freaking *freeways* collapsed and decided that a basement was a good idea — or this was an older building and the new owner got it at a bargain price *because* of the basement.

The concrete down here had all been freshly painted — taupe mostly, in the hall — but that loading bay had been through the wars. Which meant that the building wasn't new.

Wait. Why would they slap fresh paint down here, but not do anything to freshen up the loading bay?

Made me wish I knew what more of the club looked like.

More and more, though, this club — maybe specifically this *building* — was starting to feel like the reason I was here. Too much was odd about it for it to be anything less than a splinter point.

I found the employee breakroom. I didn't go in. Just looked from the doorway. Never felt it was my place to go in those breakrooms. Wasn't an employee, after all.

Saw some clothes hanging in dark green mesh lockers that had no locks. EVM strikes again. Did mean that the waitstaff was around here somewhere, which was good. And I smelled recently microwaved popcorn, which was even better. Suggested that they'd come through during our soundcheck, and I hadn't noticed because I was working.

That was all fine. Normal, even.

And the breakroom itself fit what I expected. Some store brand of soda in a machine that took quarters. Cheap candy bars in another. Kitchen area stained enough to look as though it had been the scene of canned spaghetti carnage.

Two folding card tables with folding card table chairs. Strictly garage sale veterans. Missing feet.

Nothing I needed to know in there.

Found the employee restrooms. Two, and gendered, so I only checked out the men's. Recently cleaned and bleached, bless whoever did it.

A couple of locked doors. Heavy things. Steel, with kick plates. Probably supply rooms, because they had no labels. Not even an *employees only* sign. But then, this whole area was intended for employees only. Which said something about how the EVM thought of *us*.

The hallway didn't just end, though. It had a bend to the right.

Wandering down, listening for anything closer and more concerning than the sound of my own quiet boots on the concrete, I took a peek around the corner.

No more lights down that little stretch of hall. Just shadows. The hall looked like it ran maybe another thirty feet, and ended in a door.

Thirty feet of hallway would be enough to put that door past the back walls of the only rooms I'd seen down here.

I gave my eyes a moment to adjust and started down. Nice and slow.

Felt like I was doing something I wasn't supposed to. Had that feeling of being watched. Kept expecting to trip some kind of alarm, maybe. Or for someone big to come loudly out of that door and demand my business.

Colder, down this hallway. Maybe because we were underground. Maybe all the concrete. Maybe the lack of light bulbs to add a little heat. Maybe just my own nerves.

Tough call, really.

I reached the door though, and I could smell the dust on it.

This door wasn't steel. Hardwood. Painted black, and in that dim light, I couldn't tell anything more about its look. Might've been words painted on it, but I couldn't tell.

Door was locked and deadbolted, though.

From this side.

Okay. Weirder still. I was starting to wonder if I'd walked down that set of stairs or fallen down a rabbit hole.

I cranked open the deadbolt and undid the handle lock.

Sneaking one more peek first over my shoulder, I opened the door.

Facing it was another door. Like you find in hotels with adjoining rooms.

This second door was even dustier, and locked and deadbolted from the other side.

What the hell was going on here?

I was just trying to remember if I kept lockpicks in my guitar case in this world — I did sometimes, to keep EVM's from locking us out — when I heard Greg whistle an alert.

I shut the door and looked back.

Greg's silhouette against the lights of the main hall.

"Come on, Leon," he said. "Showtime!"

8

I COULD HEAR THE DIFFERENCE BEFORE WE EVEN ASCENDED THE STAIRS to the backstage area. The low rumble of a crowd, above us. Moving. Talking. I could feel their vibrations through the concrete. Theirs, and the bass from the pre-show music.

"Gotta be a full house," Greg said, smiling. He had that extra bounce in his step he always did before a show. And he wasn't the only one. All of us were stepping a little lighter. Arms bent. Hearts beating faster. Eager to play. Eager for the crowd.

This. This moment of anticipation on the way to a stage. Everything else had been just preamble. But this, *this* was the first part of the show for us. That carbonation of adrenaline. That hungry tension.

The energy of a crowd. It's a cliché. I know. But if you've ever done what we do, you know it's more than that. It's real. I don't know if it's electricity or magnetism or just the heat of all those bodies, moving.

But it's real. And I was feeling it — *we* were feeling it — even before we reached the wings backstage.

Roadies were still busy, moving about, but I didn't know what they were doing. Well, I knew what three of them were doing — waiting to hand Greg, Stevie and me our guitars, and they got them right the first time — but I had no idea why any of the others were still moving about. What last minute things they were taking care of.

Mr. Hey Dickheads was there with his clipboard. He had a walkie in his other hand, listening to some last-minute information, but the words just sounded like static to me.

I was strapping on my Flying V. Running my fingers over the fretboard. Waiting for the signal. Waiting for the houselights to dim.

Waiting. With all the patience of an Olympic sprinter in the starting gate. Of a NASCAR driver *willing* that starter flag to move. All my weight forward. And not just mine. Greg, Stevie, Danny and I, we were all already on the same beat. Our hearts were probably even pounding at the same time.

We were one big coiled spring. Ready. So ready.

When the houselights dropped and the crowd started shouting, we could have sprinted to our places.

We didn't. Even then we were all of us pros.

Instead, we were all about the cocky swagger to our places. Danny at his drums. Greg at stage left. Stevie at stage right. And me, right there in the middle.

Danny hit a roll across his three higher toms, getting an excited burble from the crowd. His little good-luck charm. Did the same thing just before starting every rehearsal and every gig. One day it would get written about in magazines as a colorful affectation.

If we hit in this world. This strange world with a club opening in Milpitas of all places.

Someone's voice over the PA. Not mine. Not the engineer's. Not Mr. Hey Dickheads. But a guy's voice, trying to sound impressive as he introduced us.

"Ladies and gentlemen ... the Parkway Theater is proud to present ... for one night only ... the Trash! Pandas! Of the Apocalypse!"

As introductions went, it wasn't much, but it did the job. The crowd went nuts, and we felt their shouts and screams like a physical force, lifting us even higher.

Danny clicked his sticks, and the spotlight hit me for the first verse of "Pleased to Eat You" sung *a capella*.

"The wasteland is a lonely place

Never see a friendly face

And so I never leave a trace

Of anyone out to get me."

Greg came in on cue with his awesome wolf howl and in perfect sync we had all four instruments kicking into the first rhythm figure.

And then we were off and running. This was a headliner gig, so we'd be up here about ninety minutes. A little more, probably, given extra time for solos and working the crowd. Either way, fifteen songs before we left the stage to get called back for an encore.

If this were a normal gig, I'd give all my focus to that first song. Make sure the show is off on the right foot, and sucking the crowd right in along with us. First song of the set can make or break a show.

But this wasn't a normal gig. This was a new arrival gig. And to this point I only had guesswork telling me that I was here to make sure the club hit on its opening night.

So I scanned the crowd during that first song. Much as I could anyway, given the hot, bright spotlight. But I could see the guys in leather and denim — slashed or studded or both — and the girls in leather and denim and spandex, showing more skin. Long hair every-where, and half of it headbanging.

Looked like a normal crowd, for the era. And Greg was right. A full house. But if there was something special to see out there among them, I sure couldn't see it yet. So I shifted my focus entirely back into the music.

I led us straight out of the end of "Pleased to Eat You" and all the way through "Engines Revvin'" before I took my first break to talk to the crowd.

"Good evening, you perverted rejects from the wastelands," I snarled into the mic, giving the haughty kind of twisted smile.

Screams and cheers of approval. Sharper and louder up front. Where our hardcore fans were.

"You," I continued, "who've come in here to escape the dust and the wilds. To eat and drink and fuck and feel *alive*."

Louder screams and shouts for that one, and the crowd wasn't even drunk yet.

"Give everything you have tonight," I said, seeing how many joined in as I finished, "for tomorrow may not come."

Not bad. Maybe a third of the crowd shouted those words as I said them.

That line, of course, always launched us into "Tomorrow May Not Come". Not the newest sentiment — that we should celebrate being alive while we could, because death could find us at any time — but still a popular one.

I kept my wits about me then as I settled into the groove of our show. Working the crowd and working with the crowd as much as I could while playing guitar at a mic stand.

I could feel it, though. That little twist in my gut that told me that something had started. That something big — maybe the reason I was here — was underway.

When it came, I had to be ready.

9

WE WERE HALFWAY THROUGH THE SET WHEN IT HAPPENED.

The song was "Last Night Together", and though I've always hated the term "power ballad" even I had to admit it applied to this song. Slow and melodic, but with heavy chords and bass, and a vocal line about love and loss that showcased my chops.

And not just mine. The song has a lead part that Stevie just takes to a whole nother level with his solo. And that night, that solo, had to be one of his best.

He started it slow, working with the rhythm figure and telling a story about two people finding love against all odds through a series of notes that seemed to pursue each other without ever making contact...

Until they did. Then, they proceeded in harmony for a few bars before trouble, as it had to, descended on them and the solo got going for real.

It was just as Stevie was projecting that sense of trouble descending that trouble hit for real.

A fight broke out. Somewhere to stage left.

Now, I know that in a lot of circles, metalheads have a reputation as violent. But it's unearned. Most metalheads are just as friendly and easygoing as anyone else. And the percentage of exceptions, well, it's about the same rate as you'd find among any other genre of music.

And in 1990, the kind of music we were playing didn't get pits. By which I mean mosh pits, slam pits, or whatever else the kids might be calling them in your particular world. That was a phenomenon that came out of hardcore punk shows and stuck around for thrash, death metal, and other types of metal that were a lot heavier than what we were playing.

So when I noticed the sudden movement of the crowd, forming a ring to one side, I knew it wasn't a pit. Had to be a fight.

Which then begged two questions.

First, why were people rushing into it? Most times a fight broke out, that ring was set by people wanting to watch the carnage, in the fine tradition of schoolyards everywhere.

But the ring had pulled back, and people were rushing into it. From one side...

The second question, of course, was where the hell was security? I couldn't see more than a handful of yellow shirts, and none of them anywhere near the disturbance.

Of course, I couldn't see many details anyway, because of the stage lights. I tried moving around stage for a look — I didn't have a vocal line for another twelve bars, so it should've been safe — but all I could see was chaos in that circle. And over the monitors I could make out crowd noises that didn't sound encouraging.

Then I heard what could only be a scream of terror.

I tried giving Stevie an apologetic look as I hustled back to my mic, but he had his eyes closed, off in his own world of notes and music.

Soon as I got to my mic I whistled my rehearsal *all-stop*.

Even Stevie stopped mid-note.

I could hear a lot of anger and fear and noises that didn't sound human...

"Can we get some houselights and security?" I barked into the mic. "What the hell's happening out there?"

Houselights came up even as Mr. Hey Dickheads came fussily onto stage, waving his clipboard like a sign.

"What are you doing?" he screamed. "Get back to—urrk."

He got cut off when Greg grabbed the back of his shirt and yanked, pulling his collar into his Adam's apple.

I ignored him and got my first good view of what was happening.

Half the crowd — stage right — was getting shoved right and pushing back to keep their places. The middle part of the crowd caught between them and stage left, where that ring was growing, and inside it...

Maybe you thought I was kidding before, when I talked about troglodytes, but I wasn't. They're real, and they're out there, living in caves. And kind of like Wells' morlocks, over the generations they deviated further and further from mainstream humanity.

They love their drum music though, and I've survived more than one gig for them because of that little fact.

And my first thought was that these were troglodytes. They had the posture. Slumping shoulders forward. Stringy hair. Big eyes. Nails like claws.

But troglodytes, they'd never have been able to handle a place like this. Too big. Too noisy. Too many people who weren't like them.

Plus, the vibrations from the bass and kick drum would've gone a long way to keeping them cool. Sedate.

But these things looked to have been agitated by the music. And they had yellowish, waxy skin. I don't mean like any shade you'd find on a human being. Not even one with severe jaundice. This yellow was too dark. More like earwax.

Plus, they had some kind of rancid odor that was just reaching me, but still enough to make my eyes water.

No, these things weren't troglodytes. I didn't know *what* they were.

Finally, two security guards showed up and took action.

They freed Mr. Hey Dickheads from Greg's grasp.

"This is very unprofessional," Mr. Hey Dickheads said over a scream from the crowd. To one security guard he said, "I want those houselights down *now*." To me, he said, "And you *play!*"

That was the moment that I realized that the tint to Mr. Hey Dickheads' skin wasn't from liver problems.

I turned to the mic. "Security—"

Then I saw security. More security than I'd seen so far. Maybe fifty of them. And all of them were arranged around the perimeter in squads.

Keeping everyone inside.

"That second door," I said. "Down in the basement."

"They're just perverted rejects from the wastelands," Mr. Hey Dickheads said with a sickly smile. "Just like the rest of your fans. And they're here to hear you play. So *play*."

I know this sounds weird, but for a moment I could almost believe him. I've played a lot of weird gigs in a lot of weird places. And these ... whatever they were ... they weren't all that unlike some other crowds I'd played for.

I could almost believe that the screams and fighting had been a matter of shock and surprise. That it would die down, and the crowd would be just a bunch of rockers, grooving on the music.

But the screams were still coming. And now I could see blood.

10

———

THE HOUSELIGHTS WENT DOWN AGAIN, PISSING ME OFF MIGHTILY. NOW, past the stage lights, I couldn't see what was happening beyond a suggestion. Though I could hear the shouts and screams and chaos.

By now, people were getting trampled, and there wasn't much time to try to rein back something like control of this situation.

I got in Mr. Hey Dickheads' face. One security guard grabbed my shoulder. Greg knocked his arm away.

"Get those lights up and doors open," I said. "Now."

He shook his head, sallow smile on his face. "Play and I'll guarantee your safety. Don't and ... well ... I don't like your chances."

Three other security guards stepped up behind him. This close now, under the bright stage lights, I could see that they had the same tint of waxy yellow to their skin. Must've been why the yellow shirts. Minimize the number of people who'd notice.

No choice then. No reasoning. Wish I could say I took the time for some pithy statement about our fans or something, but there just wasn't time.

I hit Mr. Hey Dickheads between the legs with the body of my Flying V.

When his head came down, I let my knee finish the statement.

Greg had already punched that one security guard in the throat, and the other three on stage tried to converge on us. But they'd made a critical error.

They'd forgotten about Danny.

He bowled all three of them to the floor, while Stevie started kicking faces with his steel-toed boots.

Problem was, this was not a fight we could win. Not like this.

But I had one more card to play.

I grabbed the mic — still live, because I guess they were still expecting us to play — and bellowed, "Everyone run for the exits! Roadies! We got a code red! Repeat! A code red! We need those doors *open!*"

See, while a bunch of those security guards might've been new to the jobs — nepotism hires, I was starting to think — I'd seen those roadies at work. Setting up. Handling soundchecks. Whole nine. I knew full well that those roadies had some experience to them, which meant that their leads had to be old-school, or old-school trained.

Old-school roadies, the good ones, had done some time with traveling bands. Not necessarily the big-name acts that everyone knows, but the little bands. The ones just coming up. Just starting to make a name for themselves. The ones that are headlining, but still playing clubs that made this joint look like the Greek Theater.

And sometimes, playing gigs like those, you run across an Evil Venue Manager of the worst sort. Who didn't just cut corners, but tried to cheat the band one way or another.

So there were little codes that got spread among the gigging bands and their roadies. Most common being "code red." Which meant that the EVM was going to shaft the band out of its fee entirely.

And if the band didn't get paid, neither did the roadies.

Nothing unified bands and their roadies like an EVM trying to skip out on the bill.

"What the hell is code red?" Danny asked. I was pleased to see all four of those security guards unconscious at his feet.

"Tell you later," I said, adding the *if I can* mentally. "Every one of these people is dead unless we get those doors open. Danny, open the way. Greg, watch our backs. Stevie, with me. Try not to hurt anyone human."

"Human?" Stevie asked.

"Later," I said.

Down below the crowd was still in chaos. Some of them had gotten over by the exits, but security was keeping them at bay. Like a little bubble of space between the leather and denim and the yellow shirts.

I pointed one double-door out to Danny, and off we went.

Danny jumped down from stage and started barreling through the crowd as only three hundred pounds of drummer can, trumpeting like a stampeding elephant.

Stevie and me followed right behind him. Stevie making sure no one fucked with us, while I was yelling for people to follow us. Still trying to get as many people out safely as I could.

I think Greg had the same idea. I'm pretty sure he was trying to organize the people who followed behind us. Getting the bigger to help the smaller, that kind of thing.

How much the crowd had figured out about what was going on, I can't be sure. But I do know that they cleared a path for the bellowing drummer. So Danny got us to that double-door. Where six big, beefy security types were blocking the way, holding freaking Maglites like batons.

Looked as though they'd already clubbed some of the crowd into submission, and they were setting themselves against Danny's elephantine charge.

But Danny was no longer the only elephant in the stampede. Some of the bigger guys from the crowd had joined in. And even more important than the aid those guys could give...

A horde of angry roadies came charging to our aid.

Ah, roadies. Not all of them are big like that Viking guy earlier. But they all need some muscle to do what they do. And they looked to be as righteously furious about the thought of not getting paid as I was about this whole organized attempt on the part of the venue ownership and management to feed our fans to ... whatever those things were.

Once the melee was underway, I knew we'd get those doors open. And once some were open, others would follow.

But we were nowhere near out of the woods yet. And I had more work to do.

I grabbed Stevie. Had to yell over the tumult. *"They get the doors open. You help the exit. Organize. Right?"*

Stevie nodded. Started grabbing some people in the crowd to help him.

I grabbed Greg. *"With me."*

He nodded.

We plowed back into the crowd, heading the one place I didn't want to go.

Straight back to the slaughter.

11

―――――――

I DIDN'T HEAD STRAIGHT FOR THE MOSH PIT FROM HELL, THOUGH. No. I knew that if this was going to work, I'd need a weapon a little better than words or my Flying V. So with Greg in tow, I cut my way through the crowd towards the source of the best weapons around.

The bar.

I'm not sure what it says about metalheads that there were still about a half-dozen men and women drinking at the bar.

All around them, people were screaming and shouting and pushing for the exits. In two places I knew of, all-out war was breaking out. Some of it between security and the combined forces of the roadies, the crowd, and Danny. The rest a battle for survival between the rockers and ... whatever those things were.

Even here, where the smell of beer was strongest, the rancid odor of those things was getting overwhelming.

And yet, there were six people, drinking and talking like this was any other night at any other bar.

Rock and roll.

Trish had two helpers back behind the bar, but none of them were busy at the moment. So I had no trouble getting her attention.

"What the *fuck* is going on?" she asked.

Weirdly, I wanted to tell her. I mean really tell her. Even though she couldn't possibly have any better a frame of reference for those things than I did, and I'd end up wasting *way* too much time trying to explain.

I had to shake away the urge.

"It's a slaughterhouse," I said. "Everyone needs to get out while they can. You and your people included."

Suddenly her whole focus was on me. All business to an extent that even she hadn't been earlier. "What do you need?"

"Help us make torches," I said, nodding to the stool at Greg's feet.

Greg, god love him, might not have known what was going on, but he trusted me. He smashed that stool against the bar and broke us free a couple of legs while Trish fetched us cheap, but presumably very *strong* whiskey. Bourbon, I think, but I didn't have the attention to worry about brand names.

Meanwhile, I was tearing up the remains of my shirt — offering a small, silent apology to Steven Tyler and Joe Perry of Aerosmith, and hoped that they'd understand — to wrap the ends of those chair legs.

Soon as they were wrapped, Trish had them soaked.

One of the drinkers — a tall guy with brown ringlets down to his ribs and wearing no shirt under his leather jacket — held up his Zippo.

"Fuckin' *metal*, dude," he said, and lit our torches.

I led our way through the crowd, yelling at stage volume to get people out of my way. And those who didn't move fast enough, got prodded with the body of my Flying V. At all costs, I had to make sure my torch didn't get *anywhere near* anyone's hair. With the amount of Aquanet in this room, that could've killed everyone faster than these ... things.

Greg didn't follow behind me, though. He moved right alongside me, using his bass the way I used my Flying V, and between us we crossed the floor at a decent rate, all things considered.

I had to have been exhausted. I know I was sweating worse than the time I'd had to help push a band's van five miles through Arizona desert heat. But I was running entirely on adrenaline at that point, and thinking about a lot of things, none of which were me.

We reached the circle and the stink made me retch. Blood and offal and that *hideous* rancid odor that accompanied these waxy yellow *things*.

There were only maybe twenty of them. And only maybe half of them were fighting when we reached the circle. The others were ... feasting on the fallen.

But the ones who weren't, they were fighting the metalheads who'd practically dressed for this.

See, I wore some studs on my leather wristbands and boots. But these guys were wearing spikes. Spiked gloves. Spiked sheet metal covering entire forearms. Thick leather jackets with more studs and spikes. It was a hell of a look. And they were giving almost as good as they were getting.

But these *things*, these waxy, yellowish *things*, they had a truly ferocious level of tenacity. And they had some kind of wiry strength that went well beyond their unimpressive builds. Add to that their animalistic barking and snarling and I was just no closer to understanding what they were than I had been when I first saw them.

"Humans!" I yelled as loudly as I could to be heard over the racket. *"Make a hole for firepower!"*

I admit, I'm more than a little surprised they did. But those guys had been doing the Lord's work, holding the line for as long as they had. And most likely, they were all on the brink of collapse.

Then again, maybe they'd just responded to the word "firepower."

Either way, the two in the middle of the staggered line pulled back and Greg and I came in, torches blazing.

I caught a waxy yellow bastard in the chest. Greg caught his in the face.

Both of them screamed so loud and piercing it hurt *my* ears. And I was wearing my concert earplugs.

Got all their attention, though, and they started backing off. The humans they'd been fighting collapsed in place, which made a couple of the feasters twitch like they were about to change plates at a buffet.

A torch to the face put an end to that.

And believe me. These things didn't smell any better burning than they had before.

But then Greg and I weren't alone with the torches. Trish was beside me, one of her own burning, and the guy with the Zippo stepped up beside Greg. Flashed me the devil horns.

We formed a wall of flame between those things and the humans. Not just the living, either. We shooed the feasters away from the dead as fast as we could.

We had fire. And they didn't like that. But somewhere inside their heads, they'd figured out that they had us outnumbered. Even as they backed off, they started grunting at each other. Maybe trying to organize for a counter-attack.

But suddenly the numbers shifted.

This was in the days before cellphones. When going to a concert meant that even the nonsmokers would bring lighters, to wave during certain kinds of songs. And all the humans around us started pulling out lighters.

And that wasn't all.

All that Aquanetted hair proved to mean that there were plenty of cans of Aquanet in the crowd. And a number of women turned theirs into flamethrowers, spitting fire straight at the faces of those waxy, yellowish things.

They got the message loud and clear. The feast was over.

The inhuman things started retreating backstage.

12

I WASN'T WILLING TO RISK THAT THIS WAS A PARTIAL RETREAT. ONCE those ugly, stinky bastards began funneling backstage, I turned to the crowd.

"Get to safety! Now!"

Soon as I had some of them moving, I nodded to Greg and we started after those things.

"Where are we going?" Trish asked, to my surprise staying with us. The guy with the Zippo had peeled off to do something else.

One look at the steel in Trish's eye and I knew she had every intention of seeing this through. Just like I did.

"Down in the basement. End of the hall, there's a—"

"That door behind the door? That's where they came from?"

She smirked at my astonished expression.

"Hey," she said. "What kind of bartender would I be if I didn't know all the exits?"

Any other time, I probably would've laughed at that. But in the moment, I could only make a breathless sound, while the three of us chased these inhuman monsters toward the side stairs.

"I'll cut off their other escape," I said, and without waiting for a response I ran and jumped up onto the stage.

Just in time. Three of them were cutting toward the stage entrance. Coming my way.

I jabbed my torch at them, but they understood they had me outnumbered. And I didn't have lighters and Aquanet backups this time.

They got this crafty look to their beady black eyes. I started waving that torch back and forth. Not giving any of them an opening to charge. But I couldn't get them to back off. They started slowly spreading out.

I'd been leading with the torch in my right hand. And they kept their eyes glued to it.

So I snapped the torch at the one to my right, then thrust it at the face of the one in the middle.

The one to my left came at me. Face leading. Claws out to the sides to cut off my escape.

But that waxy yellow bastard had forgotten about my Flying V.

I swung as hard as I could one-handed and caught him in the chin so hard that...

So hard that...

Excuse me.

I caught him in the chin so hard that...

Damn. It doesn't get any easier to say this.

I caught him in the chin so hard that the sweet, walnut neck of my Flying V snapped. I think bone may have crunched too, but the sound of that walnut neck snapping on my beloved Flying V — first concert-grade guitar I'd owned in this world — it rang louder in my ears than all the shrieks and screams and shouts and ... all of it.

I can still hear that snap sometimes, in the worst of my dreams.

Anyway, that one went down, and I jammed the spike of what was left of the neck into its throat, finishing the creature off.

Maybe it was the violence of what I'd just done. Maybe it was the look in my eye after I'd done it. But the other two broke and ran flat out.

I came after them. Howling for more blood. More vengeance on the things that had ruined my gig, killed my fans, and cost me my Gibson Flying V.

I caught up with Trish and Greg at the top of those concrete stairs, with the bad guys trying for a combat retreat, but unwilling to close with our torches. And with the three of us side-by-side between those concrete walls, they had no choice but to keep backing away.

But we had a problem. Three pinch points coming up, and with some of them facing us, backing away slowly, others had fled ahead.

Some of these things could be in the bathrooms. The breakroom. The green room. Hiding. Waiting to ambush us. Make us fight on two sides at once.

We reached the breakroom first. Only one place to hide in there. Right behind the half-open door.

"They've been here," Greg said, and it was true. Clothing had been yanked down from the lockers and strewn about. Cabinets thrown open. The microwave lay broken on the floor, beside the over-turned card table.

Strangely, the chairs were still in the same places they'd been earlier.

Couldn't smell that popcorn now, though. Not under the rancid odor of those things, and the smell of the torches.

"*Fuckers*," Trish said, and I realized some of the clothes strewn about had to be hers.

"I'll check the door," I said. "You two hold the hall."

When I got their grim nods, I slammed the door the whole way open as I stepped into the room.

Something squeaked, more in surprise than pain.

The thing threw the door closed, and I set it on fire.

This one was smarter than some of the others though. It only needed a moment of jumping around in pain to drop to the floor and start rolling. Trying to extinguish itself.

I didn't waste that time.

I grabbed one of those chairs in my free hand.

"This is for my Flying V!" I yelled and swung hard. Caught it in the back.

It wasn't enough. So I dropped the torch and swung that chair with both hands until it *was* enough.

Then, panting and sweaty and shaky, I picked up my torch and opened the door again.

Trish's torch was right there.

"Whoa!" I said, backing off.

"Just making sure," she said, then pulled the torch back and I joined them in the hall.

The bathrooms were empty. So was the green room, though it was in shambles. And there was no food left, but the bottled water bottles and soda cans were spilled across the floor. Maybe not recognized as consumable.

From there, it was just a matter of time. Pushing them back, step by step, until we had them on the other side of those two doors.

"Throw your torches," I said, and both Greg and Trish gave me wicked smiles.

They threw pretty well, for burning chair legs. Caught a couple of the bastards, and got them gibbering or barking or whatever that sound was as they fled away into darkness.

With the torches down there, though, I could see farther than I could have before.

I could see that the other side of this door was stone, not concrete. And it sloped away pretty sharply. Down, somewhere under the earth.

We pulled back to our side. Closed and locked the door.

"Wish we could weld this thing shut," Trish said.

"I'm afraid that's not an option," a voice said from behind us.

A male voice. One I didn't recognize, but I knew who it was. Who it had to be. Just from the self-confident tone. That sense of being in charge.

We turned then, and I got my first look at the Parkway Theater's Evil Venue Manager.

13

I still had my torch in one hand, down in that concrete hallway under the Parkway Theater. Greg to my right. Trish to my left. All of us sweaty and exhausted. Those things banished back behind the locked door behind us.

But in front of us, the Evil Venue Manager.

He didn't look like much, but they never did. This one was ... maybe five-six, in loafers with a little lift to them. Balding. Pasty. Sweaty, but less like it was from effort and more because it came with being as heavy as he was.

Oh, he wasn't *round* or anything. But he sagged. Like he'd given up the fight with his weight back in his twenties, and a couple of decades later he'd made peace with his sloppy body.

He was wearing a suit, though. Which was weird. Most EVMs tried to dress like they belonged in the crowd. But this guy, he wore a black suit with a pale blue shirt and a dark orange tie.

An odd look. Especially with the brown belt and loafers. Like he knew he was supposed to dress up for this special night, but didn't know how to do it.

And yeah. I wasn't surprised to notice a dark, waxy yellow tint to his complexion, now that I was looking for it.

But even now, the bastard reeked of confidence. Well, that and Brut.

Man, it was just one bad smell after another in this place.

EVM hadn't come alone, which might've been part of the reason he still looked confident. He had four of his beefier security thugs behind him.

"I must say," he said, "I'm disappointed. Do you know how long I've been preparing for this night?"

"Since your first wet dream?" I asked.

"Funny," he said drily. "No, ever since the quake last year opened the way that we'd all thought closed forever. You see, our forefathers live a very hard life down below. They must scramble for every ounce of meat they can get. Makes them ... impatient, if you will."

"So you figured, hey, why not throw them a feast, then get them in a chatty mood while they're fat and happy?"

Wasn't me that said that. It was Trish. I have to say, she was handling all this a great deal better than I expected.

"Precisely." He shook his head. "Took us months just to lure them this far. And now, in one evening, you've undone years of searching. Months and months of hard, laborious work. Set us back, well, I don't know how long it will be before I can establish enough trust to try again."

"I'd apologize," I said, "except *you tried to feed us all to a bunch of goddamn ghouls!*"

"Hardly," EVM said with a raised eyebrow. "They're quite alive. Their name for themselves, well, it's difficult to pronounce even for me."

He made a barking, growling kind of sound. Closest I could come to it was Brakur.

"Lovely," I said. "But the point stands. You just tried to feed *us*, our *fans*, our *roadies*—"

"*My* roadies, thank you," EVM cut in. "You certainly didn't pay them."

"And you never intended to," I said sharply. "Hell of a way to cut your overhead."

"Yes, well, one does what one must, the economy being what it is." He shrugged. "I never intended to pay you either, but it would have looked suspicious if I hadn't offered you the standard pay-to-play deal."

"Enough chit-chat," Greg said. "It's over. So get the *fuck* out of our way."

"Oh, no," EVM said. "You have provided me with an excellent opportunity, one I do not wish to waste. You see, the Brakur are terrified of you and your torches. And it will go a long way toward their recovery from that fright if they get to eat *you*."

The security guards took a step forward.

I lowered my torch aggressively.

Greg raised his fists.

Trisha drew a freaking Bowie knife from her boot.

Who the hell *was* this woman?

But around the corner they came.

The roadies. Bruised. Bloody. Angry. And looking for the man who was supposed to pay them.

Oh, yeah. I'd told them it was a Code Red. No way they'd leave without getting paid.

And at the front of the pack, two people. Danny, looking furious and triumphant, and the guy with the ringlets, still carrying his torch. He smiled a wicked smile and threw me the horns again.

"Looks like the odds have shifted," I said with a dark grin.

The roadies bellowed a challenge and charged.

To their credit, EVM's security guards did their best. But honestly, the fight didn't take long.

14

THE ROADIES GOT THEIR MONEY. AS DID TRISH AND HER ASSISTANTS. And frankly, we could all have gotten some extra out of it — which we considered, for our pain and suffering — but Stevie suggested putting everything else we got out of EVM's safe toward a victims fund, and we all agreed.

All told, there were twelve dead among the concertgoers, and about another twenty hurt badly enough to need medical attention.

Well, to be honest, another twenty or thirty beyond that probably *should* have gotten medical attention. But youth is slow to believe in its mortality. Even after an event like that one.

Nobody called the cops, which would have surprised me at almost any other place and time. But there and then, people who rocked the hard rock / heavy metal kind of style all got the same look from cops.

Like we were trouble.

So even though we were the innocent ones here, we knew that if the cops showed up, there was too good a chance that some or most of us would be going to jail. So nobody made the call.

Oh, the cops would get involved eventually. People were dead.

Others would have to report the incidents that put them in the hospital.

But that night, as we filed out of the Parkway Theater and into the parking lot, it was just us.

The survivors.

Wasn't all that late. Maybe ten o'clock. But the club was on its own, at one edge of a shopping mall that was otherwise dead and buried.

The air was cold, after all that heat. But it smelled good. Clean smells. Tarmac and motor oil and sweat and *humanity*.

"Gear's still inside," Danny said.

Stevie and Greg were still wearing their guitars. It was Greg who first spotted what was missing from me.

"Your Flying V!"

I nodded.

"Those *fuckers*," Stevie said, with feeling. "That was a sweet guitar."

"Feels petty to complain about it right now," I said.

"We should get the rest of our gear," Danny said.

"Yeah, about that..." It was the guy with the ringlets again. The one who'd lent his Zippo and his efforts to the cause. "*Pretty* sure you don't want to go back in there."

"What do you mean?" Stevie asked. "The things are gone, right?"

"I mean right now the flames are spreading through the backstage area." Shook his head with a mock frown. "Shame about all the partying backstage. All that alcohol, with all those extension cords. Just a matter of time, really."

I heard it then, coming from inside. The roar of the flames.

"My kit!" Danny yelled, but he didn't get two steps before Greg, Stevie, Mr. Zippo and I restrained him.

"We're insured!" Stevie said, right in his face. "And paid up. Saw to it myself. The venue goes up with our stuff inside, we'll get paid." He looked at me. "Should cover your guitar as well."

I nodded grimly.

Danny nodded and we let him go.

"That whole place was a firetrap," Mr. Zippo said. "Didn't take much to get it going. And it'll look like the venue's fault. Guaranteed."

"How can you be so sure?" I asked.

"He grinned." I'm an electrical engineer. "*Nothin'* for me to spot all the weak spots."

I nodded. Sighed.

"So much for opening a new venue," Greg said, shaking his head. "Would've made a great article in BAMM, maybe even the real papers."

"Enh, it was in Milpitas anyway," Trish said, walking up. "Who the hell wants to come *here*?"

That got a chuckle out of us.

"Talk to you?" Trish asked me.

I nodded, and we stepped away while my bandmates made woo-woo sounds.

"When did you get here?" she asked me, voice low.

"Oh, we always arrive hours before—"

"No," she said firmly. "When did *you* get *here*?"

I blinked at her. She raised her eyebrows.

"Twenty minutes before soundcheck. Woke up in the loading bay." Taking a shot, I added, "You?"

"Two days ago, when they hired me for the gig." She shook her head. "Been wondering why the hell I was here. A club opening in Milpitas? Hardly enough to cause a splinter."

"Oh, I don't know," I said. "If it hit, it could've impacted the whole Bay Area metal scene."

She nodded. Smiled at me. "You had no idea about me, did you?"

I shook my head. "I thought I was the only one. Hopping around this way."

"I've been doing it for a decade or two. Not sure how it started."

"I know how it started," I said. "You solved some problem that looked small, but could've caused a splinter. Then someone asked the question."

"Yes," she said, realization spreading across her face, making her even prettier. "How would you like to make a difference? A real difference?"

I nodded. "I'd thought he meant my band."

"I'd thought he was offering me a gig at the United Nations."

"United Nations?"

"I speak six languages," Trish said.

"Think we're going to be here long?" I asked.

"Never can tell," she said.

"We're here tonight, right?" I said.

"We are," she said with a smile.

"Feel like doing something life-affirming?"

She smiled. "Thought you'd never ask."

Turning together, we headed for her car.

SIGN UP FOR STEFON'S NEWSLETTER

Stefon loves to keep in touch with his readers, and loves to keep you reading. The best way for him to do both is for you to sign up for his newsletter.

Sign up at http://www.stefonmears.com/join

If you sign up for Stefon's newsletter, you get...

- Monthly updates about his publishing and travel schedules
- His latest news, in brief, and answers to reader questions
- A free short story for signing up
- List-only offers and occasional specials
- Plus a free short story every month!

ABOUT THE AUTHOR

Stefon Mears was in pretty much all the Bay Area metal clubs, back in the day. Stefon has more than thirty books to his credit, and he never stops writing. He earned his M.F.A. in Creative Writing from N.I.L.A., and his B.A. in Religious Studies (double emphasis in Ritual and Mythology) from U.C. Berkeley. He's a lifelong gamer and fantasy fan. Stefon lives in Portland, Oregon, with his wife and three cats.

Look for Stefon online:
www.stefonmears.com
himself@stefonmears.com